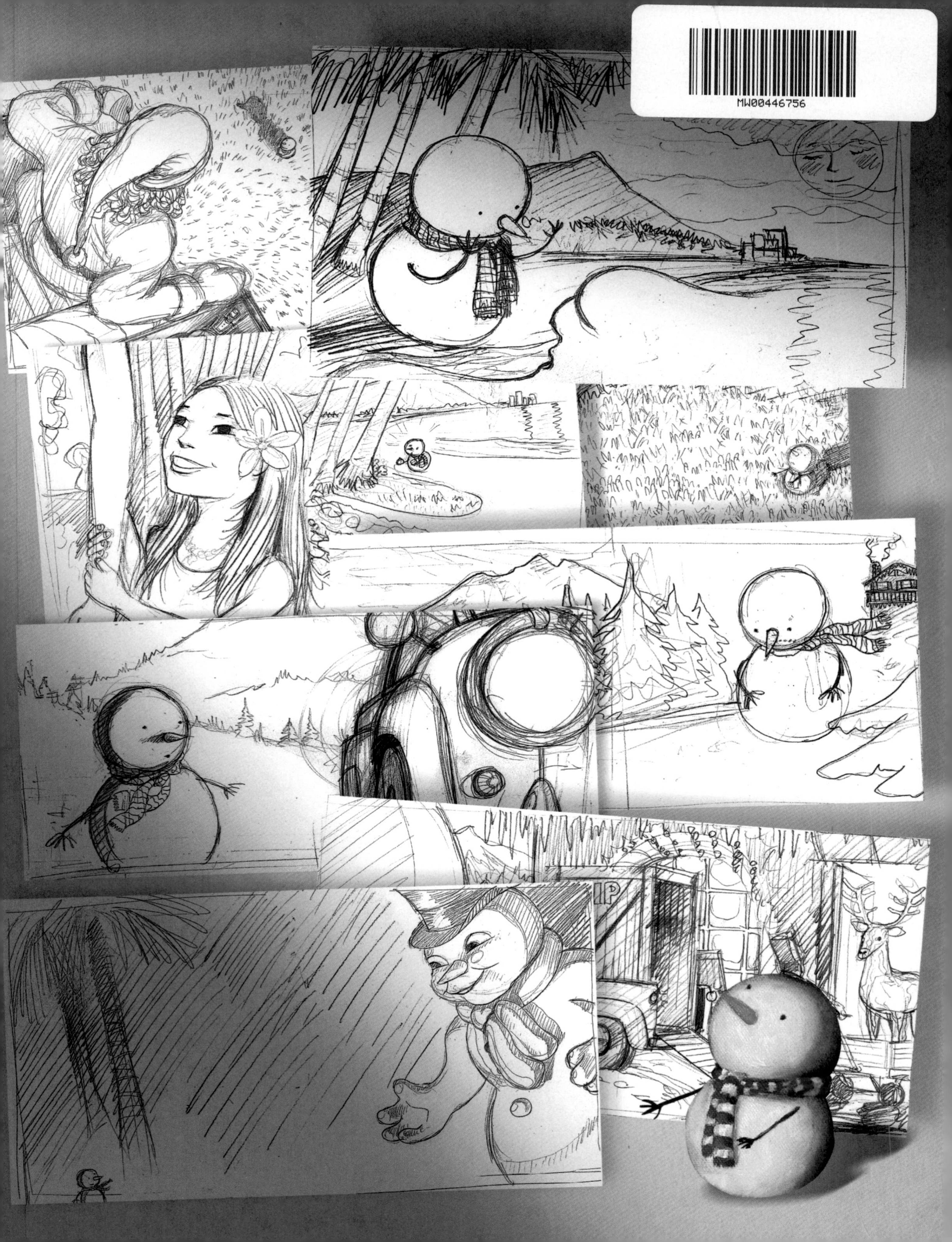
MW00446756

Library of Congress Cataloging-in-Publication Data
Lê, Christine.
The Hawai'i snowman / by Christine Lê; illustrated by Michel Lê.
p. cm.
Summary: A snowman goes on vacation to Hawai'i, getting smaller and smaller, along the way as he uses bits of himself to help others who are in need, but finally he ends up right where he belongs.

ISBN (softcover : alk. paper)
[1. Snowmen--Fiction. 2. Christmas--Fiction. 3. Hawaii--Fiction.] I. Lê, Michel, ill. II. Title.
PZ7.L4533Haw 2008
[E]--dc22

Book design: Michel Lê
First Printing, September 2008

Visit the author at

www.facebook.com/Author.Christine.Le

Written by
Christine Lê

# The Hawai'i Snowman

Illustrated by
Michel Lê

To

Charlotte and Samantha,

our wonderful daughters.

It was five days before Christmas and the children who built the snowman had gone home. The hotel was closed. The only person inside was the chef, and he was busy carving a large ice sculpture.

The snowman felt very alone standing at the windy top of the snow covered mountain.

Night came, and he looked up at the sky. He saw the way the stars shone and glittered, how the clouds were not there. He saw the moon, and then to his surprise he saw a shooting star.

"Make a wish," whispered the moon.
"Anything I want?" he asked.
"Yes," she glowed. "Anything."

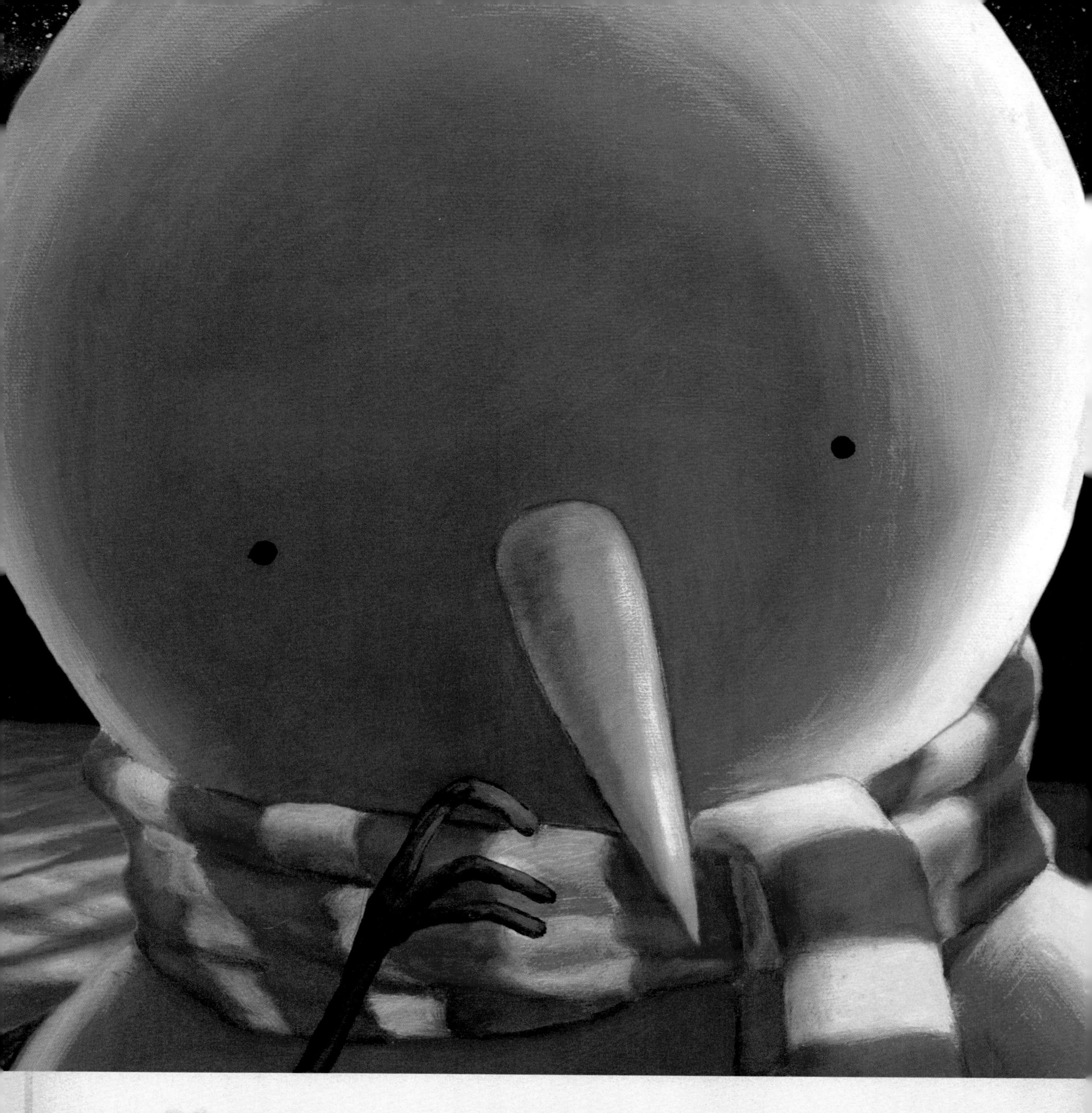

The snowman thought for a moment and then he said, “I wish to go on vacation.”

“Where to?” the moon asked.

Now, he didn’t know much about the world. He had never been to school to learn about different countries.

The children who built him were from the bottom of the mountain, and he didn't think that taking the ski lift down the slope really counted as a true vacation. In fact he had never moved from the very place where he was built.

"Tell me," said the moon, "for it will soon be day and I must go."

Then he remembered that one of the boys had said the mountain was too cold, and he wished he could go to Hawai'i.

"Hawai'i," said the snowman to the moon, who was starting to drift away.

As the moon's light faded the snowman noticed a small glow at the bottom of the mountain.
He watched as the light wound its way up the road, getting closer and closer, turning into two bright beams. A red truck stopped just in front of him.

Out of the hotel came the chef, pulling a wooden cart. On it was a beautiful reindeer made of ice. “Go with the reindeer,” said the moon from behind the mountain peak.
The snowman followed the reindeer into the truck, which was nice and cold.

“Are you going on vacation?” he asked the reindeer.
“Oh no,” the reindeer said. “I’m going to Hawai‘i for Christmas. I will stand in the entrance of a grand hotel.”

Later that evening they felt their container being lifted onto a ship. On the second day, the ocean became rough and the reindeer and the snowman slid left and right.

Some of the waves were taller than the boat.

The reindeer flew up into the air and fell back down and shattered her leg.
"I will never be able to stand," she cried, and tears froze into tiny droplets on her cheeks.

"Don't be sad," the snowman said, "I can help." And as soon as the waters were calm, he took snowflakes from his body and pressed them into the wound.

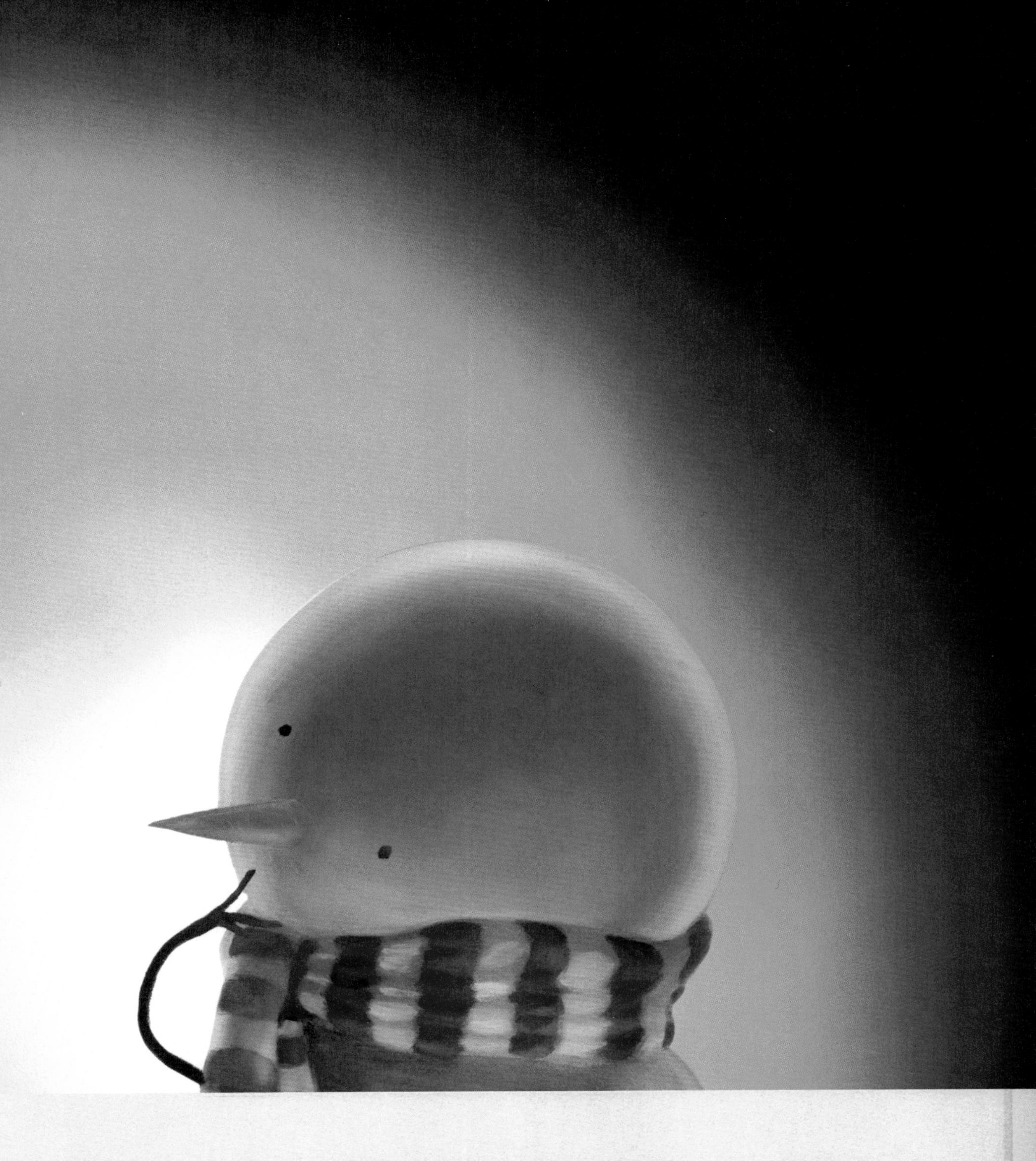

He started at the top and carefully worked his way down. By the time they arrived in Hawai'i, the reindeer's leg was strong and beautiful again.
"Thank you," said the reindeer. "Thank you."

Outside the box it was night, and although there were stars in the sky just like the mountain, the air was still and sweet. The snowman walked along the sand at the edge of the sea. It was soft and wet like the snow, but not as cold.

"I've never seen a real snowman in Hawai'i," the ocean said. "Usually they melt."

"What's melt?" he asked.

The sea lapped up to his feet and explained.

“When the day comes the sun will be hot and this will turn you into water.”
“Like you?”
The ocean looked at the snowman’s size, which was smaller as he’d used a lot of his snow to mend the reindeer’s leg. “More like a puddle,” the ocean said.
Worried and tired the snowman sat down on the grass. “I don’t want to be a puddle,” he cried out loud.

"A puddle. A puddle. A puddle," squeaked three flowers. "Can you become a puddle?"

"When it is hot," he said.

"Look at us," they squeaked some more. "No one has watered us for days. We are so thirsty we can't stand straight and our colors are turning brown. We are supposed to be bright for Christmas."

The snowman saw how the poor flowers were bent over in thirst, how the ends of their leaves were dried and crinkled, and he took some of his snow and put it around their stems. "When the day comes the snow will melt and you can drink," he said.

"Thank you," said the flowers. "Thank you."

"We want to see Frosty the Snowman," two girls shouted. He looked up. So there was another snowman in Hawai'i. "Please," they said, pulling their parents toward a trolley.

Quickly, he followed. "All aboard," the driver called, and soon they were passing a large pink hotel, and through the window he saw the reindeer standing near the entrance. She turned her face toward him, and he saw that the tears had changed into a beautiful smile.

Then they passed thousands of colored lights blinking red and green and gold. There were elves, and a Santa, and Mrs. Claus too. And finally there was Frosty. He hurried off the trolley, afraid that day was coming.

Frosty was very very big. The snowman, who had used most of his snow for the reindeer and the flowers, was now very very small. Would Frosty hear him?

But before he could even try to speak, Frosty said, "I spoke to the moon and she told me you must wait here."

"What for?" he asked.

"For an old friend of mine. He helped me once, and the moon says he wants to help you too."

Frosty pointed up to the sky, and at first the snowman thought he was pointing to the moon, but then, from out of the stars, he saw a golden sleigh pulled by nine magical reindeer.

“Santa,” the snowman shouted excitedly. “The children told me all about Santa.”

The sleigh shone in the moonlight, and the ring of bells silenced all who were close enough to hear.

Santa pulled the sleigh right up to where the snowman was standing.

"You know the true meaning of Christmas," Santa said.

"I do?"

"Yes," said Santa. "When the reindeer hurt her leg you gave what you could to help her. And when the flowers were thirsty you took your snow to make them water. You have shown great kindness. Here they call this the Aloha Spirit. You are a true Hawai'i snowman."

“But now you are afraid you will turn into a puddle?” Santa asked.
“Yes. It is nearly day. When the sun becomes hot, I will melt.”

"Then come with me," said Santa. "I have plenty of space in the sleigh. I already gave the children their presents in most of the world. I have a few more stops, and then I am going home."

"To the North Pole?"

"Yes. It is cold there, and you will not be lonely. There are elves, and reindeer, and Mrs. Claus too."

"Thank you," said the snowman. "Thank you!"
And Santa stretched out his hand and the snowman climbed into his palm.
He was very small indeed.

In fact, he was now the smallest snowman that had ever walked the earth, but he was also the one with the largest and happiest heart.

Also available on Amazon by the same author

*Kingdom of Nain*

Visit the author at www.facebook.com/Author.Christine.Le

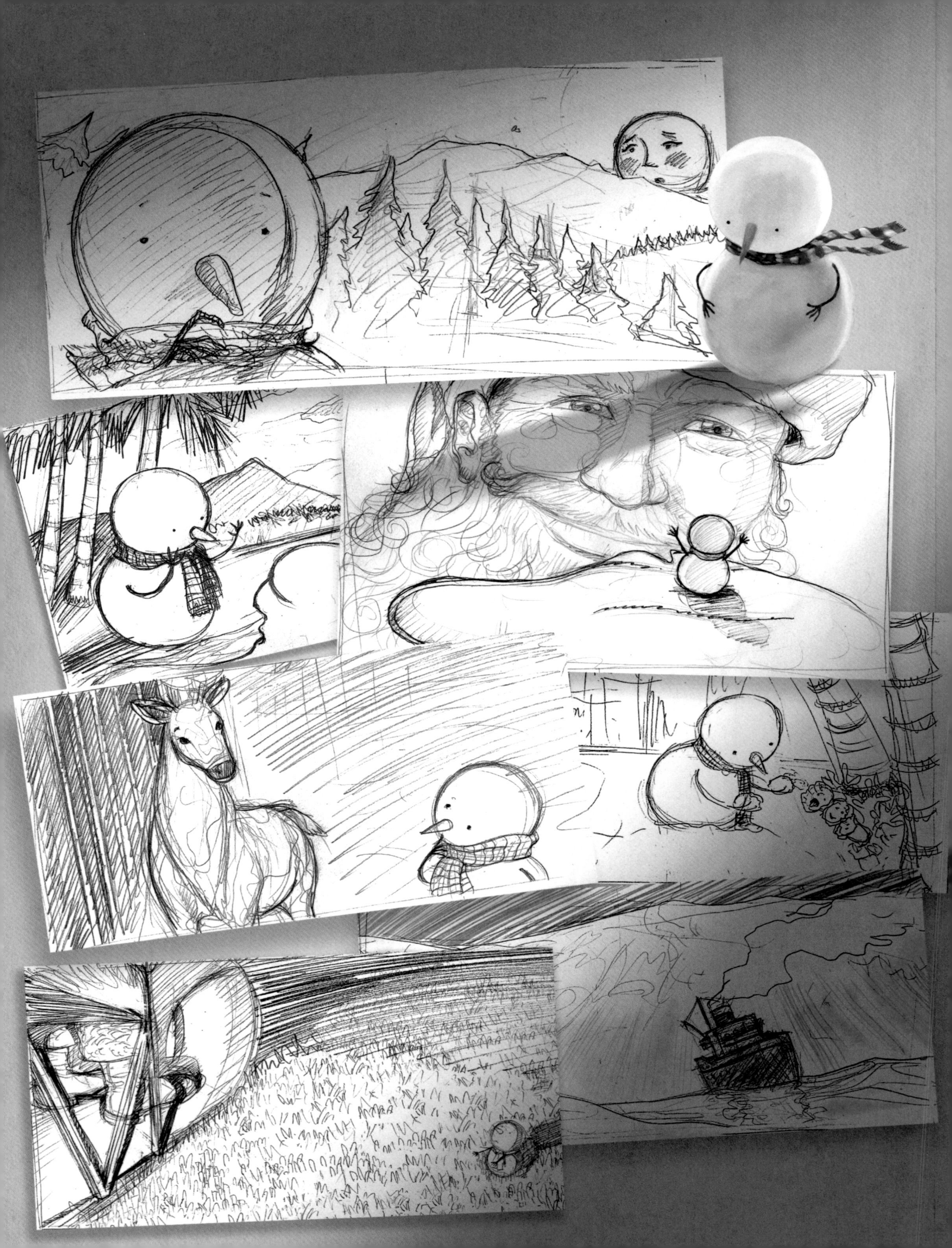

Made in the USA
San Bernardino, CA
06 December 2016